Waltham Forest Libraries

N

Please return this item by the last date stamped. The loan may
renewed unless required by another customer.

Oct 19		
16-6-22		

Need to renew your books?
http://www.walthamforest.gov.uk/libraries or
Dial 0333 370 4700 for Callpoint – our 24/7 automate
line. You will need your library card number and your
know your PIN, contact your local library.

ewal
ot

D1459359

WALTHAM FOREST LIBRARIES

904 000 00661031

**Waltham Forest
Libraries**

904 000 00661031

Askews & Holts	29-Oct-2019
PIC	£12.99
6172756	N

First published 2019 by Macmillan Children's Books
an imprint of Pan Macmillan
20 New Wharf Road, London N1 9RR
Associated companies throughout the world

www.panmacmillan.com

ISBN: 978-1-5290-1646-8

Text and illustrations based on stories and characters created by Tove Jansson

© Moomin Characters™ 2019, © Gutsy Animations 2019

Written by Amanda Li, based on the Moominvalley animation scripts by Steve Box,
Mark Huckerby and Nick Ostler

Designer: Lorna Scobie
Editor: Justine Smith

Moral rights asserted. All rights reserved

No part of this publication may be reproduced, stored in a retrieval system, or transmitted,
in any forms or by any means (electronic, mechanical, photocopying, recording or otherwise),
without the prior written permission of the publisher

1 3 5 7 9 8 6 4 2

A CIP catalogue record for this book is available from the British Library

Printed in China

Adventures in MOOMINVALLEY

Inspired by the works of
TOVE JANSSON

MACMILLAN CHILDREN'S BOOKS

Contents

NESTLED IN A BEAUTIFUL VALLEY and surrounded by forests stands the tall blue Moominhouse, where the Moomin family live. Visitors from near and far are always given a warm welcome in Moominvalley, whatever the time of day – or year . . .

Little My Moves In

. . . in which the Moomins are disturbed
by unexpected guests – among them someone
small with a very big personality

IT WAS WINTER in Moominvalley and thick snow lay on the ground. The Moomin family were tucked up in bed in the cosy Moominhouse, sleeping their deep winter sleep.

Moomintroll was having a wonderful dream. He was floating on a soft fluffy cloud next to Snorkmaiden, swooping gently through the sky when . . . BANG! He fell out of bed, and woke up.

BANG! BANG! The loud noise carried on.

"What's that? Bats?" called out a startled Moominpappa.

"Someone's knocking at the door," said Moomintroll.

"What time is it?" asked Moominmamma sleepily.

"It's only a quarter past winter!" said Moominpappa. He got out of bed and shuffled to the front door.

"My darling Moominpappa!" cried the Mymble, kissing him on the nose.

"Mymble! Er – and all your children!" said Moominpappa, eyeing them nervously.

"I thought I'd come and stay with you," said the Mymble breezily – "for a well deserved rest."

"Mymble, what a lovely surprise! Do come in," said Moominmamma. "We didn't expect anyone to come calling before the spring!"

The Moominhouse was soon in chaos. Moominpappa and Moomintroll took refuge behind the sofa, while the little ones rushed about, noisy and wild.

And what was this? Now they had found a coil of rope, and before he knew it, Moominpappa dangled helplessly from the ceiling.

"Release me at once!" he said. "But slowly!"

Moomintroll backed away and into the hall. The front door flew open with a crash. A dark shadow appeared on the wall – then a small figure stepped inside.

She was wearing a red dress and her flaming red hair was tied up in a bun. She stood and stared.

Moomintroll wasn't quite sure what to do but, as Moomins are always polite, he decided to shake paws.

"Hello there, little one," he said, holding out his paw. The small person looked at it and gave it a hard bite.

"Yow!" yelled Moomintroll. "What was that for?"

"Calling me little," she said. "Little My's my name – not my personality."

Moomintroll could already tell that Little My was going to be Big Trouble. He sidled out of the room and sprinted upstairs to the safety of his bedroom. Little My turned to the others.

"Well, what are you waiting for?" she said with a mischievous smile. "He obviously wants us to hunt him!"

With delighted cries, Little My and her siblings rushed after Moomintroll, and chased him from room to room. There was nowhere for a terrified Moomin to hide.

Moomintroll charged back downstairs and leapt onto the sofa. He hid his face under a cushion and gave an exhausted sob.

"Don't worry dear, I'm sure they won't be staying long," said Moominmamma.

"Yes – we'll be gone by Midsummer at the very latest," said the Mymble, strolling past.

"But Midsummer is months away!" wailed Moomintroll. "I'll never survive! If only Midsummer could come a whole lot earlier this year," he muttered.

"That could be arranged!" said Moominpappa. "It would be the kindest way . . ."

Soon the Moomins had transformed their winter world into a midsummer one, with artificial grass, trees and flowers. They even put their costumes on and went for a swim in the icy pond.

"I think it's working . . ." said Moominpappa.

"Why don't you just tell Mother to go?" asked Little My. "You don't have to be big to stand up for yourself!"

"Because that wouldn't be kind," said Moomintroll.

He and Moominpappa began to light a crackling Midsummer bonfire.

"Midsummer already!" said the Mymble. "We'll be on our way!"

"Must you?" said Moominpappa, trying hard to look sad.

With a loud SWOOSH, a jet of water gushed onto the bonfire. "I've heard about your bonfire," said the Hemulen fireman, sternly. "It's too early to light fires. It isn't Midsummer yet." Little My grinned happily.

The Mymble frowned. "We can forget all about leaving for a few more months!" she said.

Moomintroll climbed the stairs to his room. He flopped onto the bed.

"This is my room now!" shouted Little My, popping up from under the bedcovers. She bundled him out and slammed the door.

Moomintroll stormed downstairs and picked up Moominpappa's tool box.

"Where are you going?" asked Moominmamma, anxiously.

"To start anew!" said Moomintroll. He marched out of the house, towards the beach.

After hours of hammering and sawing, Moomintroll's house was ready for painting.

"My own private space at last," he said. But Little My turned up again, and perched on a paint pot, giggling.

"You should never build a house on sand, you know," she said.

Moomintroll's new house sank, very slowly, out of view.

"All this trouble because you can't say no!" said Little My, gleefully.

Moomintroll was furious. He grabbed Little My and pushed her into the paint pot. Then he ran – back to the Moominhouse and to his own bedroom.

"You're not getting your room back!" shouted Little My. She bounced after him. "It's my room!" insisted Moomintroll.

They burst into the house and clattered up the stairs.

There in the bedroom stood the Mymble, with her brood around her.

"Isn't this the perfect place to let my little ones run riot?" she said. "I knew you two wouldn't mind sharing."

Moomintroll and Little My sat on the stairs.

"I *could* build another house," said Moomintroll.

"*I'll* choose where to build it," said Little My. "Deal?" She shook Moomintroll's paw. And she didn't bite.

Little My chose the spot – a large smooth rock – and they got started on the new house.

"When will you be moving in, dear?" said Moominmamma, when it was done.

But Moomintroll led Mymble to the front door. "Dear Mrs Mymble," he said. "Allow me to present your new home."

"Thank you!" said the Mymble.

She followed her little ones into their new house, and then – something very strange happened. Four large flippers emerged, and the entire house rose up out of the wet sand. It was built on the back of a giant turtle! And now it began to head towards the sea.

"Good work, son," said Moominpappa.

"It's a mobile home!" called Mymble. "I've always wanted to see the world. Goodbye! I hope you won't miss me too much . . ."

"We'll manage somehow!" called Moominpappa, happily. "Bon voyage!"

But Moomintroll felt a little sad. "I'll miss having Little My around," he said.

Night-time had arrived in Moominvalley, and it was time to go to bed.

As Moomintroll settled under the covers, a familiar face peeped out, making him jump.

"Surprise!" said Little My. "I thought I'd stay. You're a bit annoying, but I don't mind too much. And did you know," she added quickly, "that it's officially spring tomorrow?"

Spring! thought Moomintroll. That could only mean one thing – Snufkin, Moomintroll's best friend, would be coming back to Moominvalley soon. And Moomintroll couldn't wait to see him again.

The Spring Tune

. . . in which Snufkin
composes a new tune to
mark the arrival of spring

Spring had come to Moominvalley. The snow was thawing, the sun shone, and all the creatures of the woods were waking from their winter sleep.

Snufkin was on the move. He walked through the woods, listening to the drip-drip-drip of the snow. He stopped, tapped his foot – and got his mouth organ out of his backpack. He was wondering if a new spring tune would come to him.

Snufkin blew a few experimental notes. But a rustling sound came from the trees . . . and Snufkin could feel a small creature watching him from the undergrowth.

"It's no good," he said. "How can I compose when I'm being watched?"

"Today's the day," said Moomintroll. "Snufkin . . . where are you?" He scanned the trees.

"I knew it!" said Snorkmaiden, angrily. "It's always the same at this time of year. You don't have time for me!"

"I'm sorry," said Moomintroll. "I didn't mean to ignore you. It'll just be so nice to see Snufkin again and hear about his winter adventures. And listen to his spring tune."

There was no reply. Snorkmaiden had stormed off. Moomintroll went back to his waiting.

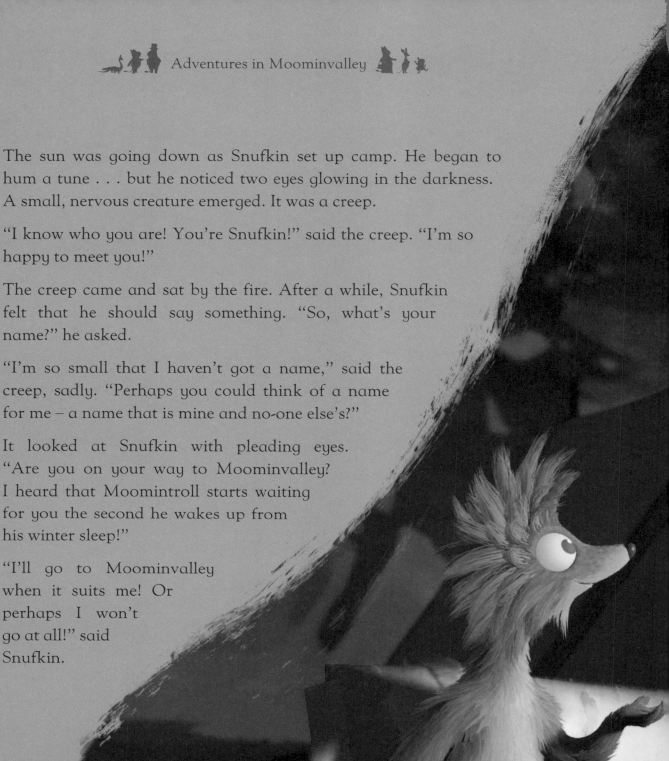

The sun was going down as Snufkin set up camp. He began to hum a tune . . . but he noticed two eyes glowing in the darkness. A small, nervous creature emerged. It was a creep.

"I know who you are! You're Snufkin!" said the creep. "I'm so happy to meet you!"

The creep came and sat by the fire. After a while, Snufkin felt that he should say something. "So, what's your name?" he asked.

"I'm so small that I haven't got a name," said the creep, sadly. "Perhaps you could think of a name for me – a name that is mine and no-one else's?"

It looked at Snufkin with pleading eyes. "Are you on your way to Moominvalley? I heard that Moomintroll starts waiting for you the second he wakes up from his winter sleep!"

"I'll go to Moominvalley when it suits me! Or perhaps I won't go at all!" said Snufkin.

"But then, won't Moomintroll be sad?" asked the creep.

Snufkin wasn't in the mood for more questions. He was just trying to compose his spring tune! He got into his tent.

"Well then," said the creep, timidly. "Goodnight."

"Wait!" called Snufkin, suddenly feeling sorry for the creep. "That name. How about . . . Teety-woo?"

The creep was overjoyed. "Teety-woo! TEETY-WOO!" it shouted. "I have a name!"

It danced away.

Night fell and Snufkin slept. He dreamt he was at the window of the Moominhouse, looking in. Moomintroll was with his new friend – Teety-woo! He had forgotten all about Snufkin.

"Moomintroll!" called Snufkin, waking with a start. But the face looking down at him was Teety-woo's.

"Have you ever visited Moominvalley?" asked Snufkin, wondering if there was any truth in his dream.

"No. I'm very busy these days," said Teety-woo. "Now that I have a name."

Snufkin smiled. "Goodbye, then, Teety-woo," he said.

Snufkin packed up his things. "I think it's time for me to go to Moominvalley to see Moomintroll," he said.

31

"Now then, about this spring tune," said Snufkin. "Something new. One part expectation, two parts spring sadness, and for the rest, just the great delight of walking alone, and liking it."

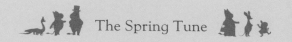

The sweet sound of Snufkin's new spring tune drifted towards the Moominhouse, where Moomintroll waited.

The Last Dragon

*. . . in which Moomintroll
learns that friends, as well as dragons,
can be unpredictable*

ONE EARLY SPRING DAY in Moominvalley, Moomintroll took a break from waiting for Snufkin. He went fishing instead. "I'm going to catch one of those little wobbly bugs," he said, lowering his jam jar into the brook.

"So you want a pet you can keep in a jar and boss around," said Little My, scornfully.

Moomintroll ignored her. And a little later, when he peered into his jar, he saw that he had caught something altogether more exciting than a wobbly bug.

"By my everlasting tail!" said Moomintroll. "It's a dragon! Just wait until Snufkin sees you!" he said, tapping the jar. The dragon gave a little growl.

"You are to be mine and Snufkin's secret, ONLY," said Moomintroll.

He rushed back to the Moominhouse carrying his prize, and sneaked past his family. He climbed up the back way to his bedroom, and he locked the door. Released from the jar, the dragon hissed at Moomintroll, and bit his finger.

"Come here!" said Moomintroll. "Come to me!"

But the dragon ignored him.

At lunchtime, Moomintroll decided to take a break from dragon training.

"Wait here and be good!" said Moomintroll. "Stay!"

He went down to join his family, passing Little My on the steep stairs.

"*Certain* people seem to be hiding secrets in mysterious glass jars!" said Little My with a frown.

"If someone wants to keep a secret, then he can," said Moominmamma mildly. "In a jar or anywhere else he likes."

But Moomintroll decided not to tell Little My about his dragon. He didn't tell Moominmamma, and he didn't tell Moominpappa either.

Just as the family were finishing their lunch, the spring tune drifted towards the house.

"Snufkin!" said Moomintroll. He rushed to meet his friend.

"Moomintroll," said Snufkin, nodding. "How was your winter?"

"Snufkin . . ." said Moomintroll, trying to look cool and calm.

"Hey, Snufkin – have you ever, um, ever come across a dragon on your wanderings?" he said.

"A dragon?" said Snufkin, raising his eyebrows. "You don't mean lizards? Or crocodiles?"

"No. I mean an actual fire-breathing dragon!" said Moomintroll.

"Never," said Snufkin. "They're extinct."

"Yes of course," said Moomintroll, bursting with his secret. "But what if they're not? What if . . . someone found the very last one and caught it in a glass jar? And what if it could spit fire, and was devoted to me – er, I mean, to the one who found it?"

"Impossible!" said Snufkin.

"But it's not!" shouted Moomintroll, hopping around in excitement. "Because I've found one! A real live dragon of my own! It's in my room, right now! Come and see!"

"It's extremely dangerous – only I can handle it," said Moomintroll proudly. He led Snufkin into his bedroom. "So, what do you think of him?"

Snufkin looked around. "I think he's invisible," he answered.

"Bad dragon!" said Moomintroll, peering under the bed. "You naughty thing, where are you?"

Snufkin looked up. There it was, swooping around the ceiling, flapping its tiny wings!

"My dragon is flying!" said Moomintroll. He grabbed a butterfly net and jumped up in the air to catch the small creature. But the dragon simply breathed out a jet of flames and burnt a hole through the net. It flew upwards and perched on the curtain rail.

"Come now, my faithful little monster," said Moomintroll, trying to tempt it down. But the dragon wasn't interested. It was looking through the window at the world outside, making a tiny whining sound.

"Hunting in the great outdoors – that's what it desires," said Snufkin. He knew how terrible it felt to be stuck inside when you wanted to be free. "You can take the beast out of the wild, but you can't take the wild out of the beast."

Moomintroll put his dragon on a lead, and went for a walk with Snufkin.

Along they strode until . . . Bzzz! A fat bee flew past and the dragon shot off like a speeding rocket.

"Help! Wait . . ." shouted Moomintroll, as he was dragged into the trees, bumping over logs and being scratched by branches.

Snufkin looked steadily at Moomintroll for a moment. Then he untied the dragon's string, and set the wild creature free.

But Moomintroll's dragon didn't fly away. Instead, the little wild creature gave Snufkin an adoring look and perched on his shoulder.

"Shoo!" said Snufkin, turning back towards the Moominhouse.

Moomintroll trailed along in the background, watching his dragon hover devotedly next to Snufkin.

*

"How sweet!" said Moominmamma at tea-time. "What's his name?"

Moomintroll sighed. "It doesn't have a name.

And it's nothing special," he said sadly. "Just a dragon."

"It'll burn the house down when it grows up," said Little My, with a scowl. The dragon lunged at her, nipping her finger. Moomintroll perked up.

"Perhaps my dragon's trying to protect me!" he said, hopefully.

But the dragon flew back to Snufkin.

"*Your* dragon?" said Little My. "Don't you mean Snufkin's?"

Snufkin quickly stuffed the creature under the tea cosy.

"Er – thanks for tea," he said. "I'll be off now."

"Interesting," said Moominpappa, studying a large book. "Says here dragons are most stubborn. Once a dragon forms a bond with its master . . ."

Moomintroll opened the door and let his dragon go.

Snufkin was fishing on the river bank, when he heard the sound of tiny wings flapping. The dragon landed next to him.

"You might be very handsome, but that doesn't mean I want you around all the time," said Snufkin. "And there's Moomintroll to think of."

But the dragon curled up in Snufkin's hat. Tiny wisps of smoke came out of its nostrils as it began snoring gently.

Snufkin looked back at the Moominhouse. There was Moomintroll, standing sadly at the window.

What shall I do? thought Snufkin.

A boat appeared, sailing down the river. At the helm was a fine-looking Hemulen. He peered at the dragon.

"What does it eat?" the Hemulen asked. "Does it bite?" (Hemulens like to know all the facts.)

"Flies, fish and this is the non-biting kind," said Snufkin. "Here, take him." And he handed his hat to the Hemulen.

"Just because I'm giving him to you, doesn't mean he's yours," said Snufkin. "Dragons will be dragons."

He pushed the Hemulen's boat away from the bank. "Bon voyage!"

Off they sailed together, a confused Hemulen with a hatful of dragon.

Snufkin watched them go.

Snufkin had just cast his fishing line into the water when Moomintroll appeared.

"Where's *your* dragon, then?" said Moomintroll.

"Haven't seen him since I left the house," said Snufkin.

Moomintroll looked surprised. "But I let him out," he said. "Didn't he fly to you?"

"No, no," said Snufkin. "Dragons – they do as they like. If they see a fat fly, they forget everything else. That's dragons for you. Not very loyal."

Moomintroll smiled at Snufkin. The two friends sat peacefully, watching the sun set slowly on the warm spring evening, the sound of their low voices drifting out across Moominvalley.

 The Last Dragon

Moominsummer Madness

*. . . in which the Moomins
go on an unexpected journey*

IT WAS A BEAUTIFUL SUMMER DAY in Moominvalley, and Moominmamma had just given Moomintroll his first bark boat of the season.

Moomintroll watched his boat spin, gently clockwise, on the water. Clockwise . . . that's good luck! he thought.

But the little boat changed direction . . . and sank. Then a drop of water landed on Moomintroll's nose. The sky turned grey, and there was a loud rumble of thunder.

Rain began to lash down on Moominvalley, and Snufkin started packing up his camp. "Snufkin! Where are you going?" demanded Moomintroll. "You've only just arrived!"

"Higher ground," said Snufkin, looking towards the mountains.

Moomintroll watched him go. "Snufkin . . . " he whispered, longingly.

But Snufkin was already out of sight.

"He's got the right idea," said Moominpappa cheerily, clambering up from the stream where he'd been measuring the rapidly rising water levels. "Perhaps we too should take cover in the mountain caves – like our noble ancestors! Rising at dawn . . ."

"Or – we could just go inside?" interrupted Moomintroll, pointing to the Moominhouse. Moominmamma would be waiting, with hot drinks and fluffy towels.

"That could work too!" agreed Moominpappa. They dashed home through the storm.

"If you ask me, this will all blow over by the morning," said Moomintroll.

"And if it doesn't," said Moominmamma, tucking him up in bed, "I'll still be here . . ."

And with that Moomintroll went to sleep.

Moomintroll opened his eyes in the morning to . . . rays of beautiful sunshine! He ran downstairs to the front door and flung it open to embrace the day.

WHOOSH! A wall of water gushed in, swirling, whirling, filling the Moominhouse. Books, plants, pencils and cushions floated past Moomintroll.

Luckily, Moomins are excellent swimmers. Moomintroll swam upwards and climbed out onto the roof. "Mamma! Pappa!" he cried.

"Good morning dear," said Moominmamma. "Did you see the note I left you, to say not to open the front door?"

"Er . . ." Moomintroll looked around him. The whole of Moominvalley was covered in water – a vast Moomin ocean.

"Good of you to join us," said Little My, perched up high. She, Moominmamma, Moominpappa and Snorkmaiden were all enjoying a rooftop breakfast.

"No more washing dishes!" said Moominmamma happily, flinging a plate into the water.

Moominpappa looked through his binoculars. A kind of house floated closer and then loomed over them.

"Extraordinary!" said Moominpappa. "The fourth wall is entirely gone!"

The house had high curved ceilings, two long red velvet curtains and a large wooden deck.

"Whatever is it?" asked Moominmamma, in awe.

"It's dry, that's what," called a voice. It was Little My, looking down at them from her rooftop perch. "So I say we jump ship!" And she was gone.

One by one, the others followed her onto the deck of their new home. Moomintroll watched sadly as his beloved Moominhouse disappeared below the water.

"I know darling. It really was such a nice house. But these things happen," said Moominmamma, kindly. "I know creatures who never get in dangerous situations. But – how miserable their lives must be!"

The new house was dark and dusty. "Poor family!" said Moominmamma. "I wonder what happened to them?"

"Let's split up and look for supplies," said Moominpappa, marching off into the gloomy interior.

"I'm sure we can make it feel like home," said Moominmamma, brightly.

Moomintroll heard a voice calling from the water. "Moomintroll, over here!" It was Sniff, sitting on the muskrat's back. "I'm going to find the plug," he called. "You coming?" and he paddled away.

"I'll take my chances here, thanks!" said Moomintroll.

Moomintroll and Snorkmaiden went off to explore. "I'll protect you," said Moomintroll as they crept down a dark corridor. There was a sudden noise from behind them. "Who's there?" said Moomintroll, nervously.

"Dinnertime!" called Moominmamma. She had found a long table, laden with food.

"To fresh beginnings!" said Moominpappa, biting into a pear. But the food was made of wax. "What kind of madness is this?" asked Moominpappa crossly. He had been looking forward to lunch.

"Ha, ha, ha!" A spooky laugh suddenly echoed around the room. Everyone jumped.

"*That* kind of madness . . ." replied Little My.

"There are lots of things one can't understand," said Moominmamma calmly. "But why should everything stay exactly as we are used to?"

"You must leave this place at once!" said the loud, spooky voice.

But Little My drew back a curtain, and they saw a large rat wearing a pair of spectacles. It was speaking into a megaphone.

". . . otherwise terrible things will happen!" cried the rat.

"Like what?" demanded Little My.

"Er – I haven't decided yet," said the rat, taken aback.

The Moomins, always friendly to strangers, set about getting to know the mysterious rodent. Her name was Emma.

"Tell us all about your amazing house," said Moominmamma.

"Fools!" cried Emma, stalking over to the stage, and striking a dramatic pose: "this is a *theatre*!"

"A theatre!" gasped her audience.

Suddenly, all the lights flickered on.

"There's a reason why this theatre is bereft of life," said Emma.

"I think we're in for a story!" said Moominpappa. Moomins *love* stories.

"I was a lowly stagehand, and I fell in love with the handsome star – Mr Fillyjonk. I did a terrible thing . . ."

The Moomins waited.

". . . I whistled at him," said Emma.

"So what?" said Little My.

"You must never whistle in the theatre!" said Emma. "It's bad luck! Dear Mr Fillyjonk had an accident – and the theatre closed. I have been alone in my misery ever since!"

With a crash, the scenery collapsed around her. The Moomins clapped. "Bravo!"

"Thank you," said Emma. "But the theatre is closed. So, kindly leave by the nearest exit. Goodbye!" And off she went.

"Do we have to go?" said Moomintroll. "I was just starting to feel at home."

At that moment, the water began to rush past the floating stage. The theatre started to spin, slowly at first, then with greater speed. The Moomins looked at each other in confusion. As the theatre turned, they realised what was happening. They were caught up in a giant spinning whirlpool!

"We're going down the drain!" shouted Little My. She was right.

Sniff sailed past. "I'm sorry Moomintroll, it's all my fault! I should never have pulled that silly old plug out!" he cried. "Paddle for it – it's your only hope!"

"We need to turn this theatre into a ship!" said Moomintroll.

Emma put on an Admiral's hat. "We've got a theatre to sail!"

Little My turned on the wind machine. The curtains billowed out, catching the breeze.

Moomintroll and Moominpappa rowed furiously – and slowly the theatre-ship sailed away and out of danger.

The flood waters began to go down, and with a crunch, the theatre hit dry land. But where were they?

"Moominvalley, apparently," said Moominmamma, softly.

There was the dear old Moominhouse – damp, but still standing.

And there was Snufkin! He was staring at Moomintroll's bark boat, still floating – anti-clockwise.

"Oh, that's just the wind, changing direction," said Moomintroll.

The two friends walked back down the valley.

The Golden Tale

. . . in which Moomintroll's tail
is the star of the show

THE MOOMINS WERE in the theatre, rehearsing Moominpappa's play. It told the story of his life, starting from when he was found, as a baby Moomin, in a box outside an orphanage.

Moominpappa was directing the play.

"Cut!" he yelled.

"Louder! Louder son!" shouted Moominpappa, into his director's megaphone.

"I'm sorry Pappa," said Moomintroll.

He was playing the part of Moominpappa – and he was finding it very difficult to learn all his lines. As he read his script, he fiddled with his fluffy tail. Clumps of hair fell out on to the floor. He walked on to the stage, more tail hairs dropping out.

"MY TAIL!" cried Moomintroll in shock, suddenly spotting his tail. It was bald! Horrified, he ran home to find Moominmamma.

"My poor darling," said Moominmamma, looking at his tail. "You have been under a lot of pressure . . ."

"What will everyone say?" said Moomintroll.

"Don't you worry," said Moominmamma. "It's nothing one of my grandmother's potions can't fix."

She gave Moomintroll a spoonful of medicine, and settled him into bed.

"Mark my words, by morning you'll be as good as new!" she said.

"Maybe even better?" said Moomintroll sleepily.

"That would be impossible!" said Moominmamma.

In the morning Moomintroll rushed to the theatre late. Something very exciting had happened overnight!

"There you are!" said Snorkmaiden, crossly. But before Moomintroll could tell her his news, she pushed him into a large box, ready for his performance as the young Moominpappa.

"Oh, what is this parcel left on my doorstep?" cried Snorkmaiden, who was dressed up and in character. "Another orphaned Moomin for me to look after! Look at his little ears and his noble nose and his . . ."

Moomintroll got out of the box.

". . . GOLDEN TAIL?" finished Snorkmaiden.

Moomintroll held up his tail. Everyone rushed on stage to look.

"I just woke up this morning and there it was!" he said, proudly. Moominpappa was delighted. "A tail of pure gold! Unique . . . just like me! Bravo, son!"

On opening night, the audience waited expectantly.

Backstage, Moominpappa handed Moomintroll a large sheaf of paper.

"Your new script!" he said. "To highlight the wonderful golden tail!"

"But . . . how will I learn all these words in time?" said Moomintroll. And then he had an idea.

The curtains came up and the play began.

"Tis I, a tragically orphaned Moomin," said Moomintroll. "I may seem ordinary at first glance – but, look closer!"

He stepped out of the box to show off his shining golden tail. The audience gasped!

Moomintroll knew all his new lines! But how?

Moomintroll had stuck his new lines all over the stage – on the backs of chairs and pinned on lampshades. Only one person noticed: Little My.

"That's cheating!" she said crossly – and she switched the wind machine on.

A gust of wind blew Moomintroll's pages away, and they flapped around the stage.

Then the scenery began to blow away. CRASH! Tables and chairs and lamps flew everywhere, and Moomintroll and Snorkmaiden clung on in the wind.

"What a show!" cried the delighted audience. "You never know what's going to happen next!"

"Interval!" shouted Moominpappa, and the curtain fell. There was a silence.

Moomintroll had had enough. He turned to Moominpappa.

"I can't be you, Pappa. I quit!"

But Snufkin pointed to the audience, still cheering and clapping.

"They LIKE IT?" said Moomintroll in amazement.

"Surprisingly – yes," said Snufkin.

Perhaps the show could go on after all! Moomintroll turned to Moominpappa.

"*You* should be Moominpappa in the play!"

"But if I'm the star," said Moominpappa, "will you be the director?"

Moomintroll thought for a moment. He picked up Moominpappa's megaphone.

"Let's make this a show they'll never forget!"

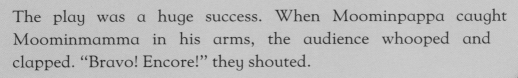

The play was a huge success. When Moominpappa caught Moominmamma in his arms, the audience whooped and clapped. "Bravo! Encore!" they shouted.

As Moomintroll stood next to the stage, Snorkmaiden noticed something.

"Moomintroll. Your tail!" she said. Moomintroll's tail was back to normal. Soft, fluffy and white – as a Moomin's tail should be.

"I'll miss my golden tail, in a way," said Moomintroll.

"Oh, Moomintroll," said Snorkmaiden. "I prefer you just the way you are."

And with that a proud Moomintroll joined his family and friends on stage, to take a final bow.

Hattifattener Island

. . . in which Moomintroll encounters
the hattifatteners for the first time

Moomintroll and Snorkmaiden were being pirates. "Walk the plank, scurvy land-lubber!" shouted Snorkmaiden, waving her wooden sword.

"Wouldn't you like to go on a real sea-faring adventure?" said Moomintroll, rather rashly.

"Like your Pappa?" said Snorkmaiden. "When he sailed away with the hattifatteners and discovered their mysterious island? We could go right now!"

"Well, the water is a little choppy today," said Moomintroll, nervously. "And we need to plan . . ."

He didn't notice that Little My, hidden in their picnic basket, had already cast off the boat and they were floating out to sea.

A dot appeared in the distance, bobbing around. It looked like a far-away boat.

"A hattifattener boat!" said Moomintroll.

There was nothing for it.

"Follow that ship, me hearties!" shouted Moomintroll, and they sailed out into deep water.

"There it is!" called Moomintroll as the distant sail came closer. But it wasn't a hattifattener boat at all. It was just an old driftwood raft, and then there was a rumble of thunder and dark clouds began to gather.

"Let's ride out the storm on that little island over there," said Moomintroll, pointing to a remote piece of grey, rocky land.

They reached the shore and the pair climbed out of the boat. The island was bleak and desolate, but by now Moomintroll was enjoying their advenure.

"Isn't it lovely! Our own little slice of paradise," he said, unloading the hamper. "You find a cosy cave, and I'll build us a camp. Then we can eat our picnic!"

The hamper was surprisingly heavy. And when Moomintroll opened it, out popped Little My!

"She's eaten all our food!" protested Snorkmaiden, scowling.

"Oh, you'll be fine," said Little My, with a loud burp. She grabbed a torch and skipped off to explore the island.

Snorkmaiden had started to pick flowers for her hair. "Perhaps don't pick too many," said Moomintroll mildly. "They could be rare . . ."

But Snorkmaiden went off to look for something shiny in which to admire her reflection.

It was getting dark. Little My had circled the entire island and now she was bored.

There was a rustling sound from the bushes. Little My switched on her torch and peered into the darkness. The torch flickered and went out. Flat batteries!

The sound got louder. A small white tube-shaped creature appeared. It bumped into a nearby tree and made a fizzing noise, like the crackle of electricity.

Hmm, thought Little My. She tipped the batteries out of her torch and slid it over the white creature, screwing the cover down. Ta-da! The torch shone.

"I'm full of bright ideas!" she said, just as Moomintroll and Snorkmaiden came along, looking for something to eat.

"Look!" said Little My. She shone her torch on three more little white figures.

"Hattifatteners!" gasped Moomintroll. They watched as the hattifatteners wandered around, aimlessly. Whatever they touched lit up with an electric FIZZ! Moomintroll remembered what Moominpappa had once told him: "They wander the world, never stay anywhere for long and don't seem to care about anything."

A hattifattener brushed against Moomintroll's leg, giving him an electric shock. "Ow!" said Moomintroll. "Let go!"

"I'm not scared of these lollipops!" said Little My. The hattifatteners formed themselves into a line. They began to buzz and vibrate. Little My's torch began to vibrate too, as an unknown force pulled her towards them.

"Mine!" said Little My, clinging on to her torch. "Let me go!" she cried, but it was no use. Moomintroll watched in horror as Little My was whisked away into the darkness.

Behind him, Snorkmaiden had caught sight of something shiny glinting through the trees. She climbed up to an object, hanging from a wooden pole. It had a polished glass face with hands and little pictures, a little like a clock. Snorkmaiden looked into the glass and patted her fringe. "So beautiful," she murmured.

More hattifatteners approached her. "Get away from me!" she shouted, stamping her foot. She grabbed the shiny thing and hurried off with it. Now it was hers!

"Little My?" cried Moomintroll, then . . . "Snorkmaiden?"

He thought for a moment. "Snorkmaiden. I must look for her first . . . then *she* can rescue Little My," said Moomintroll.

Moomintroll searched everywhere for Snorkmaiden. Then he made his way back to the cave.

"I've been decorating!" announced Snorkmaiden.

The cave was adorned with all kinds of flowers, nets and driftwood.

"What's that?" asked Moomintroll.

"That's my new mirror!" said Snorkmaiden. "I found it!"

Something small bumped against Moomintroll's leg. He looked down. Little My!

"All the hattifatteners wanted was their battery back," she said, holding up the empty torch.

"You used a hattifattener as a battery?" said Moomintroll, astounded.

Click! Click! The hand on the shiny clock was moving. A little counter spun, until it landed on a number – two hundred and fifty-nine – and then a small picture – of a hattifattener! A flash of electric lightning lit up the cave.

"Er – I think we may have some visitors," said Moomintroll, nervously.

Outside the cave were hundreds of hattifatteners! Two hundred and fifty-nine, to be exact.

"What do they want NOW?" asked Little My.

"I think I know," said Moomintroll, looking at the shiny thing. "Snorkmaiden?"

Snorkmaiden was hiding in a sleeping bag. "Make them go away!" she begged.

The hattifatteners began pouring into the cave. Little My jumped into a teapot and Moomintroll backed away. The hattifatteners kept on coming. As they brushed against Snorkmaiden there was a crackling sound and a burning smell. Her fringe was singed!

Moomintroll grabbed the shiny thing from the wall and edged his way out of the cave, followed closely by the little white creatures and Little My.

"My mirror!" said Snorkmaiden. "But it's not yours, is it?" said Moomintroll crossly.

Escorted by hordes of swaying hattifatteners, Moomintroll climbed up to the wooden pole. It looked empty. So he hung the shiny thing onto the pole. "Time to leave," he said.

"All that trouble for a clock!" said Little My.

"It wasn't a clock," said Moomintroll. "It was some sort of barometer."

He and Little My watched the strange hattifattener ceremony from behind a rock.

Hundreds of hattifatteners bowed to the shiny clock solemnly, then bowed again. As the lightning flashed, they began to shine and glow, like hundreds of light bulbs.

Moomintroll thought of something Moominpappa often said: "Perhaps the hattifatteners gather together to greet the storm. Or, maybe they create it. Perhaps we will never know – and that's the way it should be."

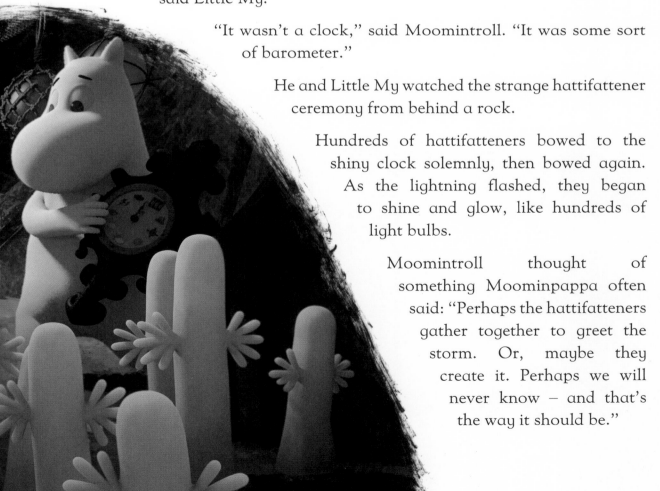

Morning came. It was time to go home. Moomintroll, Snorkmaiden and Little My jumped aboard the boat.

Moomintroll looked at the fringeless Snorkmaiden, picked up her pirate bandana and gently placed it on her head.

"That looks better," he said. "Hair looks so untidy, anyway, don't you agree?" She smiled. Moomintroll always knew the right thing to say.

They cast off the ropes, and Little My opened the hamper to see if there was any food left. She felt around inside and pulled out – a hattifattener! It buzzed – and gave Little My an electric shock.

"Ow!" she shouted and tossed it into the ocean. It immediately swam to join the disappearing hattifattener boats.

Everybody laughed – except Little My.

"Shocking!" said Moomintroll happily.

He watched the hattifatteners' boats sail away.

"Looking for the next great storm," said Moomintroll. He wondered if he would ever see them again.

Snufkin and the Park Keeper

*. . . in which Snufkin sows
some hattifattener seeds
and causes mayhem*

SNUFKIN WAS WALKING ALONG, playing a happy tune on his mouth organ, when, CLANG! He walked into a hard iron railing. Snufkin frowned. He hated to feel enclosed.

Snufkin picked up the sign on the railing. "Private Park. Keep Out," he read, slowly. "Do not enter without permission."

"Whose permission?" said Snufkin. "The forest belongs to us all!"

He looked through the railings to see a hemulen Park Keeper, clipping the bushes. I knew it! he thought. It had to be a hemulen!

Snufkin needed a distraction. He went fishing.

He cast his line into the river, and immediately caught something.

88

It was a work-basket. A small figure was curled up inside.

"Don't be afraid," said Snufkin.

"I'm not even afraid of ants!" said Little My.

They sat together companionably by Snufkin's campfire.

"It's not that I don't like people," said Snufkin. "It's just – every now and again – I need my space. I *will* go back to Moominvalley," he said, "but first I need to settle an account with a villain."

"How?" said Little My.

"I'm not sure yet," said Snufkin. "All I know is, a few tools would be useful."

"Just as well I arrived in a work-basket then!" said Little My.

Snufkin looked in the basket. "Well found, young Mymble!" He put some strange white seeds in his pocket. "Come with me."

When they arrived at the park railings, Snufkin pointed at the signs.

"No running. No hopping. No skipping – and definitely no fun!" he said, angrily. He looked at the Park Keeper, still gardening, and felt for the seeds in his pocket.

"These are hattifattener seeds, you know."

"What?" said Little My. "I almost ate one of those. It could have burst out of my stomach!"

"Don't worry," said Snufkin, laughing. "They will only grow into hattifatteners if they are sown on Midsummer's Eve . . .

. . . which just happens to be – tonight!" He tossed a handful of seeds through the railings.

Small white blobs began sprouting on the lawn. Two round eyes popped out from the top of each one. Then two little paws sprouted. There was a loud rustling, and a strong smell of sulphur.

"They're especially electric when new-grown," said Snufkin happily.

"Huh?" said the Park Keeper. Hundreds of hattifatteners swarmed towards him. The buttons on his uniform began to shoot sparks. His ears lit up. His hair crackled and his nose began to glow!

"Help!" he cried, dancing about, sparks shooting everywhere. Nearby, a group of little creatures watched in amazement.

"He's shining like a full moon!" cried Snufkin in delight.

The Park Keeper turned and ran out of the park gates – followed by the hattifatteners.

"And that's that!" said Snufkin. "Now to liberate the land!"

He began pulling down all the Park Keeper's signs, one by one.

"Time for a bonfire!" he said, throwing the signs into a big pile. The little creatures gathered round to watch him. They tugged at Snufkin's sleeves and tried to hold his hand.

"What are they?" asked Little My.

"Woodies," said Snufkin.

They looked up adoringly at him.

"But I'm not used to children," he said. "I don't even know if I like them!"

The woodies snuggled into Snufkin.

"Well," said Little My, "they seem to like you!"

Snufkin tried to shoo the woodies away, but they clung to his legs and started to cry. So he gave up, and decided to take them for a walk.

They came across the Park Keeper's cottage. There was no one home – but the door swung open, so Snufkin took the woodies inside.

"Every now and then I need my space," said Little My, wickedly, as she left. She had spotted a plume of smoke and skipped off to investigate it.

Moomintroll and Snorkmaiden had been looking for Little My, when they found a big pile of wooden signs in the park.

"Perfect for a Midsummer bonfire," said Moomintroll, lighting the wood. A plume of smoke drifted upwards.

Just as Little My got there, the Park Keeper arrived with a hemulen Policewoman. Little My hid behind a plant pot and watched.

"They're the culprits! Burning my signs!" he shouted.

"I suppose I'll have to throw you in jail now," said the Policewoman with a sigh.

"But . . ." said Moomintroll.

Too late. The Policewoman walked off, a Moomin under each arm.

Snorkmaiden and Moomintroll sat gloomily in the prison cell.

"This is a fine jail," said the hemulen Park Keeper, "I like the sturdy steel bars."

"To be honest," said the Policewoman sadly, "I don't much like locking people up. I prefer wide-open spaces – like the flower fields I used to run through in my distant youth."

"Well I'm off home to make up some new rules . . ." said the Park Keeper darkly, and he stalked off, still buzzing and sparking.

The Policewoman sat down and began to crochet.

"Excuse me, Ma'am," called Snorkmaiden. "Are those slippers you are making?"

"Slippers!" said the Policewoman. "Perhaps I could make you some!" She opened the door to the cell.

Little My, who had seen her friends being taken, ran back to the cottage to tell Snufkin.

"Moomintroll, and Snorkmaiden . . ?" said Snufkin.

"Yes," said Little My. "They're on their way to the local slammer!"

Snufkin, Little My and the woodies rushed to the prison and climbed onto the roof to peep inside. A loud squeal rang out from below.

"Our poor friends are being tortured!" said Little My.

"There's no time to waste!" said Snufkin. He jumped down and the woodies swarmed after him. Whump! They landed in a big heap.

The Policewoman was measuring Moomintroll and Snorkmaidens' feet.

"Hold still!"

"That tickles!"

"Ha, ha, hee . . . Snufkin! What are you doing here?" said Moomintroll.

Then the Park Keeper turned up again, shocked to see the prisoners out of their cell.

"Lock them up this instant!" he said.

"They're innocent," said Snufkin. "And *I'm* here to pay the penalty."

"He electrified me!" shouted the Park Keeper. "Sentence him at once! And make it harsh!"

"Excuse me," said Moomintroll, looking at the woodies. "I think Snufkin's punishment should be to write out 'Strictly Forbidden' five thousand times. To replace the signs he tore down."

"It's a fair sentence," said the Policewoman, handing Snufkin a pile of paper.

Snufkin sighed, picked up a crayon and started writing. All the woodies picked up crayons too.

"The little ones are helping!" said Snorkmaiden.

"There. Five thousand signs. Done!" said Moomintroll, happily.

"You know," said Moomintroll, "the park turned into a wide-open space. And the jail turned into a sign-smothered park. Perhaps you two hemulens should swap places?"

That is exactly what they did. The next day, the Park Keeper was in his jail – and the Policewoman took over in the park. She sat in a deckchair contentedly, the woodies playing at her feet.

Snufkin smiled. "They're in good hands," he said. "But I think I'll miss having all my little children. I almost started to enjoy the responsibility."

"Almost . . ?" said Moomintroll.

And where was Little My? Nobody knew. "I wouldn't worry about her," said Snufkin. "Little My can take care of herself."

Monster Fish

. . . in which Moominpappa and Moomintroll go fishing and catch more than they bargained for

I T WAS AN UNUSUALLY HOT SUMMER in Moominvalley, and the plants in Moominmamma's garden were all dried up. The Moomin family was hungry.

Moomintroll and Moominpappa took their boat out to sea, hoping to catch something for dinner. "Father and son, working together, as it should be!" said Moominpappa. They cast their lines and waited for a bite.

A loud shout from Moominpappa made Moomintroll jump.

"A school of fish! Hundreds of them!" He pointed to a large silvery shape in the water. "But it looks like – one gigantic fish!"

A huge fish leapt out of the water, its mouth open wide.

"It's the Mameluke!" shouted Moominpappa. "The biggest fish that ever swam the seven seas!"

The Mameluke dived downwards. And Moomintroll was dragged down with him.

Moomintroll opened his eyes. He was under the sea. He let go of the line – but too late. The Mameluke was coming! Moomintroll swam as fast as he could, but – GULP! The mighty Mameluke swallowed him whole!

Moominpappa came to the rescue. He leapt onto the monster, threw a rope around it, then hauled it onto the beach.

"Give me back my son!" he yelled, pulling the rope tightly. The Mameluke opened its mouth and gave a great belch. It spat Moomintroll out onto the sand – along with a large wooden crate.

Then the Mameluke whipped its tail, burst free of the rope and jumped into the sea.

Moomintroll and Moominpappa dragged the big crate up to the house ". . . And so, alas, the legendary Mameluke got away!" said Moominpappa, finishing his account and waving his arms with a flourish.

He opened up the crate to find hundreds of seeds.

"Ooh," said Moominmamma, scooping up a pawful. "Not like any seeds I've ever seen before!" She went off to plant them. "Now we won't have to eat any creatures – we'll have tropical fruit all day long!"

"But there *was* no giant fish!" protested Moomintroll. "The crate just floated past and we brought it home!"

"I guess that's why I'm the storyteller of the family!" said Moominpappa, proudly.

"I always get a headache when it's about to rain," said the Muskrat, that afternoon. Sure enough, heavy grey clouds came rolling in – and rain fell on Moominvalley.

Coiled green vines began to grow. Moominmamma's seeds had sprouted!

Little My went to have a closer look. "Watch out. They're killer plants!" warned Moomintroll.

One of the vines slid along the ground like a snake and wrapped around Little My's foot.

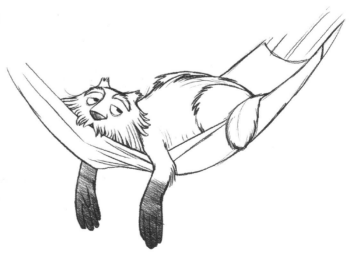

"Run for your life!" shouted Moomintroll.

"I am not afraid of salad!" said Little My, stamping on the vine.

There was a rumbling sound and the ground began to shake. Little My flew up into the air as the vines suddenly burst upwards, growing incredibly fast.

Green tendrils began creeping over the Moominhouse. Slithering vines came in through the windows and leaves covered the furniture. The garden was a writhing jungle. Moomintroll stood on the crate, like a raft in a green ocean, wondering what to do.

"You'll have to jump in and sort this mess out," said Little My, floating back down to the ground.

"That's the answer!" said Moomintroll. And he dived headfirst into the foliage.

Moomintroll forced his way through the twisting tropical vines and went down the steps into the cellar. He grabbed a pair of garden shears, then made his way upstairs to Snorkmaiden's bedroom.

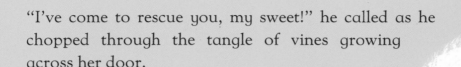

"I've come to rescue you, my sweet!" he called as he chopped through the tangle of vines growing across her door.

"My hero! You've saved me just in time!" said Snorkmaiden, coming out and giving Moomintroll a big hug.

Now Moomintroll was fighting his way to Moominmamma's room. He would rescue her too!

"Sorry old chap – I was here first," said Moominpappa, who was pulling the coiled green vines away from her bedroom door.

"But, Pappa, this is my story. I'm the hero!" said Moomintroll.

"Let me do it, son," said Moominpappa, who'd almost got the door open. "Your mother could be in great danger!"

Moominmamma rushed out. "Is this my bit of the story?" she asked. And she gave a scream.

"Quickly, dear, close the door!" she cried.

But it was too late! Rearing up behind her was a large plant. An angry Bush Beast!

The Moomins were trapped. All except for Moomintroll. He grabbed a long vine that was trailing from the Bush Beast and twisted it around the ceiling fan.

"Pull the cord, Little My!" he shouted. "Why me?" protested Little My. But she did what she was told and WHISSSHH! The fan whizzed around, and the Bush Beast was chopped into hundreds of pieces.

". . . And that's how I saved Snorkmaiden and fought the Bush Beast," said Moomintroll. He could be the storyteller of the family too! Moominmamma and Snorkmaiden clapped their hands together. "That was lovely!"

"Ridiculous," said Little My, crossly.

There was a rustling at the window. The real jungle, grown from Moominmamma's seeds, really had grown so high it covered the Moominhouse!

"But the vines are drooping," said Moominmamma. The sun was going in, and the plants were dying.

"The story is finished," said Snorkmaiden.

"Back to the boring old truth," said Moominpappa, sadly.

"So why don't we make up a new ending?" said Moomintroll. "Let's finish this story together!"

The family settled back down to listen.

"We were trapped . . . there was no way out," began Moomintroll. "The vines were wrapping themselves tightly around the Moominhouse. Soon the walls began to bend inwards!"

"We were about to be squeezed like toothpaste from a tube!" said Moominpappa.

"Then Moomintroll spotted a way out," added Moomintroll. "He ripped a board away from the fireplace and everyone scrambled up the chimney and onto the roof.

But the killer plants weren't letting them get away that easily. The Moomins looked down in horror as more Bush Beasts began coiling up onto the roof!"

"Luckily Moominpappa realised that plants had their own natural predator," said Moominpappa. "With the river full again after the rain – the bigger ocean fish could swim up-river!

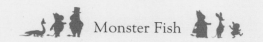

A huge wave came rolling down the river – and with it came the Mameluke! The giant fish launched itself out of the water towards the house and gulped down the vines as if they were spaghetti. The Moomins watched in amazement as the green Bush Beasts were devoured." Moominpappa paused.

"So – because I let the Mameluke swim away, it came to help us in our hour of need!" said Moomintroll. "It leapt back into the river – and gave a friendly wave of its fin. Then it headed back to the sea. I'll never forget that final wave . . ." he finished.

"Well done, son," said Moominpappa, clapping Moomintroll on the back. "Great ending!"

"Thanks Pappa," said Moomintroll. "I couldn't have done it without you."

"Yes," said Moominpappa. "We finished the story, father and son, working together, as it should be!"

Night of the Groke

... in which a mysterious grey
creature glides into Moominvalley

MOOMINPAPPA WAS IN THE MOOMINHOUSE KITCHEN, gloomily defrosting the freezer, while Moominmamma wiped down the table.

"We shouldn't be stuck inside cleaning all day!" announced Moominpappa, sweeping Moominmamma into his arms. Moominmamma gave a giggle.

"Let's head to the beach and light a fire!" said Moominpappa. "Fish for our supper! It's the wild, free life for us, my darling!"

"You'll be fine, won't you dear?" said Moominmamma to Moomintroll, a little later. "I'm sure we'll be back by the morning. There's plenty of jam in the cellar. Just be your brave little self . . ."

Moomintroll waved goodbye to his parents.

"Don't worry about me, I can survive for one night!" he said, shutting the door.

Moomintroll stood in the dark house. I'll be fine, he thought.

But just in case, he thought he might ask his friend Sniff to come over.

"Why am I here again?" asked Sniff.

"Because I need someone to help me get some jam from the cellar," explained Moomintroll. "Plum jam."

"Ah, well, if it's plum jam . . ." said Sniff.

The pair looked down into the cellar. "It's very dark and . . . cobwebby," said Sniff.

"We just . . . run down, and grab the jam," said Moomintroll. "Ready? One. Two. Three!"

A few minutes later, Moomintroll was sitting on the front porch eating jam. He was covered in cobwebs and trembling all over.

"D-d-does jam attract giant forest ogres?" asked Sniff, nervously.

"There are no monsters in Moominvalley," said Moomintroll.

"Except this one!" said Sniff. He hopped along a trail of huge footprints nearby – still clutching his jam. Moomintroll took a closer look. "I'll get Pappa – he'll know what to do," he said.

"But wait," said Sniff. "Just imagine if we captured it. We might get a big reward – then we could buy a yacht – or some roller-skates!"

"We'd be heroes . . ." said Moomintroll. A picture came into his head of everyone clapping as he received a medal for bravery.

"You're right Sniff! Let's catch ourselves a monster!" he said.

By nightfall, Moomintroll and Sniff were hiding behind a bush. "I hope Mamma won't miss her vegetable patch too much," said Moomintroll. They had spent hours in Moominmamma's garden setting traps and digging a pit to trap the big-footed monster.

They waited for the monster to arrive. Time passed – and Sniff fell asleep. Then something moved in the darkness.

"Wake up, Sniff," whispered Moomintroll. "It's here!"

There was a thud, thud, thud . . . footsteps approached!

"Run!" said Moomintroll.

They ran – and fell straight into their own pit.

The trembling pair looked up from the bottom of the pit to see – Snufkin's smiling face!

"What were you two hiding from?" he asked, pulling them out.

"A giant forest ogre!" said Moomintroll.

"It's got very big feet," said Sniff. "Look!"

Snufkin looked at the large footprints. "I made those!" he said, "from these shoes I found." He pointed to his own feet. He was wearing a huge pair of shoes. "To see what life is like in someone else's shoes," he explained.

"And what's it like?" asked Moomintroll.

Snufkin kicked off the shoes. "Uncomfortable!"

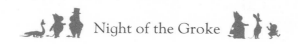

Snufkin turned to walk away.

"Wait! We're coming with you!" said Moomintroll, glancing around nervously. "We're scared!" said Sniff. "We're *hungry*," said Moomintroll.

They huddled round Snufkin's campfire while he cooked a pot of stew.

"There are no monsters in Moominvalley," said Snufkin.

"The only thing you really need to fear, is fear itself. That, and . . . the Groke!" Moomintroll and Sniffs' eyes opened wide.

"She's a mysterious silent grey shadow who haunts the wilds," said Snufkin. "She brings the icy-cold with her wherever she goes. Her very presence could freeze your heart solid. You certainly don't want to meet her on a dark night – like tonight."

"Why is she so awful?" asked Moomintroll.

"Maybe she isn't, really," answered Snufkin. "Perhaps she just reflects our own fears. She's a misunderstood creature alright."

He finished his stew and got into his tent. "Sleep well!"

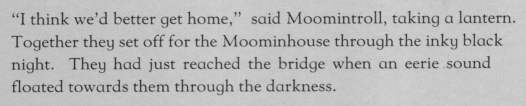

"I think we'd better get home," said Moomintroll, taking a lantern. Together they set off for the Moominhouse through the inky black night. They had just reached the bridge when an eerie sound floated towards them through the darkness.

"Mooaaan!" It was a terrible, mournful sound.

"W-what was that?" whimpered Sniff.

There came another desolate moan, then a strange grey creature drifted over the bridge towards them, leaving a frozen trail behind it. It had big staring eyes. As it glided across the bridge, the stream froze.

"The Groke!" said Moomintroll.

"Run!" cried Sniff. So they did.

"Snufkin! Wake up, it's the Groke!" shouted Sniff and Moomintroll.

"Quick, inside," said Snufkin, undoing his tent flap. He could see the Groke getting closer. Snufkin turned off the lantern. "Keep quiet," he said.

"Moooan!" whispered the Groke, coming right up to the tent. The trio huddled inside and watched, terrified, as their breath froze to a chilly mist and shards of ice crept up the outside of their shelter.

The Groke moved away from the tent. They peeped outside and watched her slide in the direction of the beach.

"She was attracted to the light!" said Moomintroll.

"We were lucky. I just hope no-one is sitting outside by a camp fire tonight," said Snufkin, solemnly.

"Mamma! Pappa!" cried Moomintroll, jumping up.

"We'll help you warn them," said Snufkin. They set off for the beach, slipping and sliding and spinning all the way down, along the Groke's frozen trail.

They landed in a heap. "Look, a frozen rock pool!" said Sniff, picking up a big flat sheet of ice.

"How can we put the fire out before she gets there?" said Moomintroll.

"With that," said Snufkin – pointing to Sniff's sheet of ice.

"I'm the fastest runner!" said Sniff, clutching his ice. "I'm going to save the day! All by myself!" And off he ran.

*

Moominpappa and Moominmamma were having a lovely time sitting by their glowing campfire.

"This is the life!" said Moominpappa.

Sniff appeared, panting hard. "Hello," he said. He threw his ice onto the fire and, with a sizzle, it went out. "Goodbye!" said Sniff – and he ran off.

Moominpappa and Moominmamma stared at each other. "Curious creature, that Sniff," said Moominpappa.

Moomintroll and Snufkin were swinging their lanterns around, trying to get the Groke's attention. Now the fire was out, the Groke turned around and glided towards them.

"I know what to do," said Moomintroll, as the Groke got closer. He looked round the beach and picked up a large piece of driftwood. He placed his lantern onto it, then launched it into the sea. The Groke saw the drifting light and began to follow it.

"Moooan!" As the Groke slipped past Moomintroll towards the sea, he couldn't help looking into her huge sad eyes. He shivered. "I suppose she's looking for a little warmth in her life," he said, feeling sorry for the bleak creature. "I wonder if she'll ever find it?"

A final "moooaan" echoed around the shore, as the Groke disappeared from sight.

"Goodbye, Groke," said Moomintroll.